EACH PEACH PEAR PLUM

In this book
With your little eye
Take a look
And play 'I spy'

EACH PEACH PEAR PLUM

Janet and Allan Ahlberg

SCHOLASTIC INC.
New York Toronto London Auckland Sydney

Each Peach Pear Plum
I spy Tom Thumb

Tom Thumb in the cupboard
I spy Mother Hubbard

Mother Hubbard down the cellar
I spy Cinderella

Cinderella on the stairs
I spy the Three Bears

Three Bears out hunting
I spy Baby Bunting

Baby Bunting fast asleep
I spy Bo-Peep

Bo-Peep up the hill
I spy Jack and Jill

Jack and Jill in the ditch
I spy the Wicked Witch

Wicked Witch over the wood
I spy Robin Hood

Robin Hood in his den
I spy the Bears again

Three Bears still hunting
THEY spy Baby Bunting

Baby Bunting safe and dry
I spy Plum Pie

Plum Pie in the sun
I spy . . .

. . . EVERYONE!

ISBN 0-590-41081-4

20 19 18 17 16 15 14 13   1234/0

Printed in the U.S.A.   23